Puss in Boots

Illustrated by Carmen Saldaña

BONNEY
PRESS

Published by Bonney Press,
an imprint of Hinkler Books Pty Ltd
45–55 Fairchild Street
Heatherton Victoria 3202 Australia
www.hinkler.com.au

BONNEY
PRESS

Illustration: Carmen Saldaña
Text: Katie Hewat
Design: Paul Scott and Pooja Desai
Editorial: Emily Murray

ISBN: 978 1 4889 0472 1

Printed and bound in China

PUSS IN BOOTS

Once upon a time there was a poor young man who owned nothing but...

a *very* clever cat.

One day, as the young man sat eating his poor meal of bread and water, the crafty cat hatched a cunning plan.

'Master,' he said, 'Give me a pair of boots and your bag and I will make all of your dreams come true.'

Now the young man, being entirely without imagination, thought his cat was referring to his lifelong dream of eating a whole goose in one sitting.

So with his last few coins, the young man bought the cat a pair of cat-sized boots and gave him his only bag.

Off went the cat to the field. First, he began by luring a large hare from its warren and sweeping it up in his sack.

Then he swung the sack over his shoulder and began on his way to the royal palace. The cat was very pleased with his perfect plan, and he *whistled* while he walked.

Once the cat arrived at the palace, he was taken before the king who was in the middle of eating his lunch. With a deep bow, the cat presented the hare as a gift, stating that it was from the marvellous Marquis of Carabas.

The king was delighted, as roasted hare was among his favourite meals. He replied excitedly with a jumble of words the cat couldn't understand, as the king was **gobbling** down a giant turkey leg.

Next, the cat used his wiles to catch two big, *juicy* partridges in the cornfield.

Again, the cat *whistled* his way to the palace and made a present of the partridges to the king. 'I say, it has been too long since I've had such a fine meal as these birds will make,' said the king with a satisfied grin.

His majesty was so pleased with his gift that he rewarded the cat with a gold coin. The cat left the palace clutching the coin to his chest and **purring** with pride.

One day shortly after, the cat learned that the king was to take a carriage ride along the riverside with his beautiful daughter, the princess.

Seeing an opportunity to progress his plan, the cat asked his master to take a bath in the river. While he was bathing, the king's carriage passed by and the cat cried out, 'HELP! The Marquis of Carabas is drowning!'

The king, seeing the faithful cat who had brought him delicious gifts, ordered his guards to stop and help.

The cat hid the young man's rags under a nearby rock and told the king that thieves had stolen his master's clothes. So the king ordered his guard to fetch a fine suit for the Marquis of Carabas to wear.

The young man was very puzzled by what was taking place, but happily accepted the fine clothing and the king's kind invitation to join him and the princess on their drive.

The cat marched on ahead of the carriage until he met some people working in a meadow that was owned by a cruel ogre.

The cat chatted happily with the workers but, before leaving, warned them, 'The king will soon pass by. You must tell him that the Marquis of Carabas owns this land, or the ogre will be **very angry**!' The frightened folk did as they were asked.

'A very fine field indeed!' said the king, as he offered the young man some tea cake.

The cat continued on ahead until he met a farmer who was harvesting corn in another field owned by the ogre.

The cat chatted pleasantly with the friendly farmer before giving him the same warning he had given to the workers.

So when the king passed by, the man told him, 'The Marquis of Carabas owns this corn, Your Majesty.'

The king was very impressed with the handsome marquis and his wealth.

Eventually the cat arrived at the cruel ogre's castle. It was well-known that the ogre had *magical powers*, and the cat was counting on this to complete the final piece of his plan.

'I have been told that you have a gift,' said the cat. 'They tell me that you can change yourself into any creature you choose, such as a lion. **Surely** this cannot be true?'

'It is true! I'll prove it to you,' said the proud ogre, and he turned himself into a **growling** lion.

The cat got such a fright that he tried to scramble up a nearby cupboard, which was rather awkward because of his boots. When he saw the ogre had finally returned to his normal form, he carefully climbed down.

'I'm very impressed!' said the cat. 'But I have also been told that you can change yourself into a small animal, such as a mouse. Surely, though, *that* is impossible?'

'IMPOSSIBLE?' roared the ogre. **'Watch and see!'**

The ogre turned into a tiny mouse and began to run around the room. Grinning a mischievous grin, the cat watched the mouse for a few moments, then quickly pounced and ate him up!

When the king's coach arrived outside the castle, the cat said, 'Welcome to the castle of my Lord, the Marquis of Carabas.'

'*What?* My Lord Carabas!' cried the king. 'Does this fine castle belong to you too?' After a quick glance from the cat, the young man agreed that the castle was in fact his own.

The cat then led the marquis and his guests through to the Great Hall where the servants, happy to be rid of the cruel ogre, had laid out a grand feast.

During the meal the young man, with the help of his trusty cat, charmed both the king and the princess, and soon the princess was completely in love.

The king was so impressed by the marquis's riches that he insisted that the marquis marry his daughter the very next day.

They lived ***happily ever after***, and the cat became a great lord. He never had to chase mice again; although sometimes he chose to, just for fun!